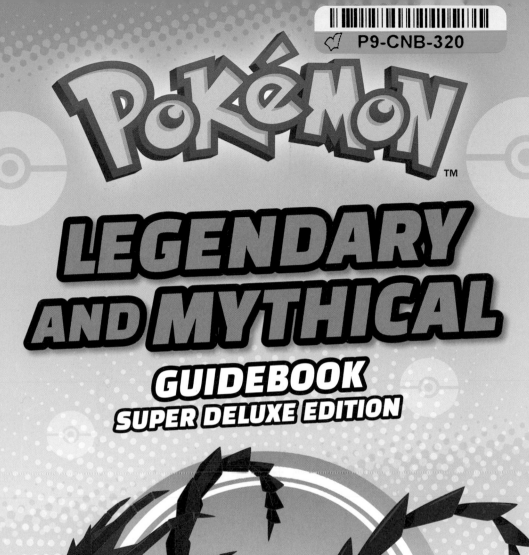

POKÉMON™

LEGENDARY AND MYTHICAL

GUIDEBOOK
SUPER DELUXE EDITION

BY
SIMCHA
WHITEHILL

SCHOLASTIC INC.

Photo © Shutterstock.com.

ISBN 978-1-338-79533-2

10 9 8 7 6 5 4 3 2   22 23 24 25 26

Printed in the U.S.A.   40
First printing 2022

Book design by Cheung Tai

CONTENTS

MEET THE LEGENDARY AND MYTHICAL POKÉMON!

The incredible Legendary and Mythical Pokémon you'll discover in this book are straight out of the pages of Pokémon legends. They're incredibly strong, far beyond many other very skilled Pokémon—and that is why they have had so much influence. They are Pokémon who have used their power to shape history and, in some cases, the world.

These Pokémon roam Kanto, Johto, Hoenn, Sinnoh, Unova, Kalos, Alola, and Galar. They are so rare that very few people have ever caught a glimpse of one of them. But we're about to give you an inside look. So what are you waiting for? Turn the page and meet them all!

LEGENDARY & MYTHICAL POKÉMON OF KANTO

THE LEGENDARY

LEGENDARY POKÉMON

ARTICUNO

FREEZE POKÉMON

Height
5' 07"

Weight
122.1 LBS.

Type
ICE-FLYING

Articuno is known as the Freeze Pokémon, and it can really ice out a foe. This Legendary Pokémon is so powerful that it can fly just by waving its long ribbon tail.

When Articuno flaps its wings, the air turns chilly. This Legendary Pokémon often brings snowfall in its wake.

When Ash and his pals were on their way to the Battle Frontier, they found themselves in the middle of a snowstorm on a warm, sunny day. When they looked up, they realized it was all because of Articuno!

MOLTRES

This Legendary Bird can really heat up the weather—and the battlefield! If you spot Moltres, it means winter is done and spring is on its way. Moltres might mean a change in season, but one thing never changes: fire always follows the wishes and whims of this Legendary Bird.

When Moltres gets hurt, some say it dives into an active volcano and heals itself by bathing in lava. This Legendary Pokémon can give off flames and control fire.

Because of its ability to create an inferno, Moltres's fire ignites the torch at the Pokémon League in Kanto. Ash wanted to be a torchbearer carrying Moltres's flame to the battlefield. He was able to carry the flame, but Team Rocket set up a sinkhole to trap him and take the torch. Fortunately, the president of the torch committee had kept a lantern with Moltres's flame burning, just in case. Even contained in a lamp, Moltres's flame was so powerful that it relit the torch and blasted off Jessie, James, and Meowth, too!

LEGENDARY POKÉMON

FLAME POKÉMON

Height
6' 07"

Weight
132.3 LBS.

Type
FIRE-FLYING

ZAPDOS

When a bolt of lightning hits Zapdos, its power increases. This Legendary Pokémon can bend electricity to its will.

When the weather doesn't call for thunder-storms, Zapdos recharges at a mystical lake at the top of a mountain near Blackthorn City. Years ago, during a rainstorm, an ancient temple possessing a powerful crystal was buried at the bottom of the lake. The crystal's powers seeped into the water, and it draws Electric-types like Zapdos to recharge in the magically strong lake currents.

Ash once brought Pikachu to heal in the lake's banks. After Pikachu's health was restored, Team Rocket swooped in and stole the mythical crystal. Zapdos used all its energy to rid the lake of Jessie, James, Meowth, and their power-sapping machine. But the crystal was accidentally blasted off, too!

Ash and Pikachu battled Team Rocket and re-turned the crystal to the lake. But even back in its underwater home, the crystal had lost its luster. Zapdos was still weak, so Pikachu bravely trans-ferred a huge Thundershock to restore Zapdos's power. The mighty Electric Pokémon regained its strength and reenergized the crystal.

LEGENDARY POKÉMON

ELECTRIC POKÉMON

Height
5' 03"

Weight
116.0 LBS.

Type
ELECTRIC-FLYING

MEW

Happy-go-lucky Mew is fun to be around, but that doesn't mean you shouldn't take it seriously. This small pink Pokémon plays a big role in Pokémon genetics.

It is said that within Mew's cells rests the entirety of the Pokémon genetic code. This Mythical Pokémon can turn invisible to keep others from noticing it.

Mew is connected to the universe in a way that is unlike any other Pokémon: It is very sensitive to the environment. When the delicate balance of nature is disrupted, Mew is affected.

Because of its great power and the knowledge it possesses, Mew is a frequent target for villains. Mew's life has been in danger on more than one occasion.

MYTHICAL POKÉMON

NEW SPECIES POKÉMON

Height
1' 04"

Weight
8.8 LBS.

Type
PSYCHIC

11

MEWTWO

Scientists created Mewtwo by manipulating its genes. If only they could have given it a sense of compassion . . .

Mewtwo is amazingly powerful but also extremely dangerous. Humans created Mewtwo's body, but they failed to give it a heart.

LEGENDARY POKÉMON

GENETIC POKÉMON

Height
6' 07"

Weight
269.0 LBS.

Type
PSYCHIC

MEGA MEWTWO X

MEGA MEWTWO Y

LEGENDARY & MYTHICAL POKÉMON OF JOHTO

HO-OH

When Ho-Oh's feathers catch the light at different angles, they glow in a rainbow of colors. Legend says these feathers bring joy to whoever holds one.

On Ash's first day as a Trainer, he and Pikachu were caught in a huge thunderstorm. When it cleared, their incredible friendship was solidified. A rainbow appeared in the sky, and Ash thought he saw a Legendary Ho-Oh fly by.

But even a Pokémon that symbolizes so much light and joy can experience darkness. Once upon a time, an evil king of ancient Pokélantis tried to harness Ho-Oh's special power to conquer the world. Instead, Pokélantis was completely destroyed, and the king's spirit was trapped in an orb. When Ash and his pals stumbled on the ancient ruin of Pokélantis, the evil king's spirit decided to possess Ash. But Ash's will was so strong that he was able to snap out of the spell.

In celebration of Ash's victory over the evil king, Ho-Oh flew across the sky. Seeing the Legendary Pokémon again brought back sweet memories of Ash's first days as a Trainer.

LEGENDARY POKÉMON

RAINBOW POKÉMON

Height
12' 06"

Weight
438.7 LBS.

Type
FIRE-FLYING

MYTHICAL POKÉMON

TIME TRAVEL POKÉMON

Height
2' 00"

Weight
11.0 LBS.

Type
PSYCHIC-GRASS

CELEBI

Celebi traveled back in time to come to this world. According to myth, its presence is a sign of a bright future.

Celebi can travel across, warp, and change time. However, it is said that Celebi will only appear in times of peace.

Celebi is also directly connected to nature. It has a special bond with forests and plays a role in protecting the environment.

LUGIA

Lugia can knock down a house with one flutter of its enormously powerful wings. For the safety of others, this Legendary Pokémon lives at the bottom of the sea.

Lugia is the great guardian of the sea. But its greatest strength might be its amazing telepathy—it can send its thoughts into the minds of others without saying a word.

Ash and his pals met Lugia and its baby when Team Rocket joined forces with Butch and Cassidy to capture baby Lugia for Dr. Namba. Ash and his pals stepped up to save the small but powerful Pokémon, but both Lugia and Ash's crew wound up getting captured, too. But Ash refused to give up. First he gained Lugia's trust, and then he called on Pikachu to help fend off Dr. Namba and his evil team. Together, they were able to free both themselves and Lugia.

LEGENDARY POKÉMON

DIVING POKÉMON

Height
17' 01"

Weight
476.2 LBS.

Type
PSYCHIC-FLYING

THUNDER POKÉMON

Height
6' 03"

Weight
392.4 LBS.

Type
ELECTRIC

RAIKOU

When Raikou roars, the air and land shudder. This Legendary Pokémon moves with lightning speed.

This Pokémon's bark is not just a scare tactic. It has the skills to back up its booming growl. Raikou is as fast as lightning, and it can fire zaps off the thundercloud-like mane on its back. Because of its connection to weather, you're mostly likely to see Raikou during a lightning storm. But it will be hard to spot because it flashes through the air with incredible leaps.

ENTEI

Where there's smoke, there's fire. In this case, the smoke that billows off Entei's back is definitely a warning. So beware: Entei's Fire-type attacks burn hotter than lava.

People say that Entei came into being when a volcano erupted. This Legendary Pokémon carries the heat of magma in its fiery heart.

Ash and his pals, amazingly enough, spotted Entei in action when a Trainer challenged the wild Pokémon to a battle! Although Misdreavus was confident Mean Look would trap Entei, the powerful Pokémon slipped away easily. Entei was gone in a flash, but its stature left a lasting impression on Ash and his friends.

LEGENDARY POKÉMON

VOLCANO POKÉMON

Height
6' 11"

Weight
436.5 LBS.

Type
FIRE

LEGENDARY POKÉMON

AURORA POKÉMON

Height
6' 07"

Weight
412.3 LBS.

Type
WATER

SUICUNE

Suicune can clear pollution from lakes and rivers. This Legendary Pokémon's heart is as pure as clear water.

When Suicune gets close to a dirty pool, the water instantly washes over it, leaving it clean and renewed. Since its special gift is so helpful in maintaining the delicate balance of the environment, Suicune is said to travel on the north wind, racing around to see where it is needed. And whether it is nature, people, or Pokémon that need its help, Suicune is always there.

Ash witnessed one of Suicune's amazing rescue missions. In fact, Ash was the one rescued by this Pokémon! When he and his friend Paige floated away with a few Drifloon, they were trapped in a bad storm. Luckily, Paige's little sister, Gabby, knew exactly where to find Suicune. Gabby asked Suicune for help, and it leaped right into action. She hopped onto Suicune's back, and the two swooped in to save Ash and Paige from a disastrous fall down a mountain. But before Ash got the chance to thank the Aurora Pokémon, it had already continued its patrol.

LEGENDARY & MYTHICAL POKÉMON OF HOENN

DEOXYS

From the crystal on its chest, Deoxys can shoot out laser beams. This highly intelligent Pokémon came into being when a virus mutated during a fall from space.

Deoxys has an incredibly intelligent mind—it just isn't inside its head. The crystal in its chest is actually its brain. Deoxys is connected to the Northern Lights, and it appears with the auroras.

On their way to Pewter City, Ash and his friends spotted an unusual aurora. Then their PokéNavs and Poké Balls went on the fritz. They noticed a flock of Altaria and Swablu flying around strangely. So Ash and his friends investigated the electromagnetic disturbance. Their investigation led them to the site where Deoxys's meteor crashed. There they found the Mythical Pokémon, cold and scared and alone in its new land. But with the help of its newfound friends, Deoxys returned to its Normal Forme. The Mythical Pokémon was so happy to have made a few pals in its strange new world, it decided to set out on a journey to make even more!

MYTHICAL POKÉMON

DNA POKÉMON

Height
5' 07"

Weight
134.0 LBS.

Type
PSYCHIC

ATTACK FORME

SPEED FORME

NORMAL FORME

DEFENSE FORME

JIRACHI

MYTHICAL POKÉMON

WISH POKÉMON

Height
1' 00"

Weight
2.4 LBS.

Type
STEEL-
PSYCHIC

This Mythical Pokémon is said to sleep for a thousand years at a time. But when it wakes up, it can make anyone's dreams come true!

According to myth, if you write your wish on one of the notes attached to Jirachi's head and then sing to it in a pure voice, the Pokémon will awaken from its thousand-year slumber and grant your wish.

Once it's awake, Jirachi will spend a whole week ensuring all the wishes on its notes come true. Then it will return to its slumber. But don't think Jirachi is completely unconscious. If it finds itself in danger, it will fight back and destroy a foe without even opening its eyes. Nothing can disturb Jirachi when it's in a deep sleep!

KYOGRE   **PRIMAL KYOGRE**

KYOGRE

Legends say that Kyogre is the sea personi-fied. When it channels the full power of nature, it can raise sea levels with mighty storms. This Pokémon often clashes with Groudon.

Kyogre is known for having the strength to bring about storms so great, they raise the sea level to new heights that completely swallow land. An ancient legend tells of a time when Kyogre awoke from its deep sleep at the bottom of an ocean trench and brought an unbelievable storm. Massive tidal waves and heavy rain flooded the land. So you may be grumpy when you wake up in the morning, but you've got nothing on this Legendary Pokémon!

LEGENDARY POKÉMON

SEA BASIN POKÉMON

Height
14' 09"

Weight
776.0 LBS.

Type
WATER

PRIMAL KYOGRE

SEA BASIN POKÉMON

Height
32' 02"

Weight
948.0 LBS.

Type
WATER

LEGENDARY POKÉMON

CONTINENT POKÉMON

Height
11' 06"

Weight
2,094.4 LBS.

Type
GROUND

PRIMAL GROUDON

CONTINENT POKÉMON

Height
16' 05"

Weight
2,204.0 LBS.

Type
GROUND-FIRE

GROUDON

PRIMAL GROUDON

GROUDON

Legends say that Groudon is the land personified. When it channels the full power of nature, it can expand the landmass with eruptions of magma. This Pokémon often clashes with Kyogre.

Weighing in at over one ton, Groudon is quite possibly the heaviest Legendary Pokémon. And it likes to throw its weight around! The Continent Pokémon has the ability to use its hot magma to evaporate the ocean and expand the land. According to legend, Groudon fell into a deep sleep after an intense battle with Kyogre.

RAYQUAZA

Legends say the ancient Pokémon Rayquaza flies through the upper atmosphere and feeds on meteoroids. It's known for stopping the endless battles between Kyogre and Groudon.

Rayquaza has a never-ending appetite for doing what's right. It's the only one who can stop Kyogre and Groudon from fighting and restore order. No one is quite sure when the battle between them began, but Rayquaza is said to be hundreds of millions of years old. Can you imagine how big a birthday cake would have to be to hold that many candles?

RAYQUAZA   MEGA RAYQUAZA

LEGENDARY POKÉMON

SKY HIGH POKÉ ON

Height
23' 00"

Weight
455.2 LBS.

Type
DRAGON-FLYING

MEGA RAYQUAZA

SKY HIGH POKÉ ON

Height
35' 05"

Weight
864.2 LBS.

Type
DRAGON-FLYING

EON DUO

LATIOS

Latios can project images into someone else's mind to share information. When it folds its forelegs back against its body, it could beat a jet plane in a race through the sky.

Latios can understand people when they speak, but it is particular about whom it opens up to. It will only converse with caring Trainers. And Latios would rather use its ability to reason than its might. Latios does not like to fight.

Ash had the rare opportunity to take on the battle-shy Latios. In the semifinal round of the Sinnoh League, Ash was matched up against Tobias. Tobias battled Latios next against Ash's Sceptile, and with one great Giga Impact, Sceptile was unable to battle.

Next, Ash called on Swellow. But Latios quickly ended the round with Luster Purge. Then Ash called on Pikachu. Latios's Light Screen cut the strength of Pikachu's attacks in half. Pikachu unleashed a combination of Volt Tackle and Iron Tail so strong that it matched the intensity of Latios's Luster Purge. The sheer force of their attacks left both Pikachu and Latios unable to battle. Tobias was declared the winner in the match against Ash, but Ash was proud of his pal Pikachu for his incredible flair in battle with the Legendary Latios.

LEGENDARY POKÉMON

EON POKÉMON

Height: 6' 07"

Weight: 132.3 LBS.

Type: DRAGON-PSYCHIC

MEGA LATIOS

EON POKÉMON

Height: 7' 07"

Weight: 154.3 LBS.

Type: DRAGON-PSYCHIC

LATIOS   **MEGA LATIOS**

LATIAS

MEGA LATIAS

LATIAS

Sensitive and intelligent, Latias can pick up on people's emotions and understand what they're saying. The down that covers its body can refract light to change its appearance.

You don't have to say a word to Latias. It can read your feelings telepathically. So if you've come to cause trouble, beware. Latias will sense it coming, ruffle its feathers, and let out a shriek so high-pitched that it will intimidate even the toughest opponent.

LEGENDARY POKÉMON

EON POKÉMON

Height: 4' 07"
Weight: 88.2 LBS.
Type: DRAGON-PSYCHIC

MEGA LATIAS

EON POKÉMON

Height: 5' 11"
Weight: 114.6 LBS.
Type: DRAGON-PSYCHIC

THE LEGENDARY

LEGENDARY POKÉMON

ICEBERG POKÉMON

Height
5' 11"

Weight
385.8 LBS.

Type
ICE

REGICE

Created during an ice age, Regice's body is frozen solid, and even lava can't melt it. It can lower the temperature of the air around it by several hundred degrees.

Regice's entire body is made of an ancient ice so cold, it's impossible to melt. It lives in a state of deep freeze at -328 degrees Fahrenheit.

HOENN TRIO

LEGENDARY POKÉMON

REGIROCK

Regirock's body is made entirely of rocks, and these rocks were recently discovered to be from all around the world. It repairs itself after battle by seeking out new rocks.

If this Legendary Pokémon is damaged during battle, it can fill in the gap with any rock it finds.

ROCK PEAK POKÉMON

Height
5'07"

Weight
507.1 LBS.

Type
ROCK

REGISTEEL

LEGENDARY POKÉMON

IRON POKÉMON

Height
6' 03"

Weight
451.9 LBS.

Type
STEEL

Registeel isn't actually made of steel—it's a strange substance harder than any known metal. Ancient people sealed it away in a prison.

After living underground for thousands of years, the metal on Registeel's body became so compressed that researchers aren't quite sure of what exactly its body is composed. Amazingly enough, the leading theory is that the metal in Registeel's body cannot be found anywhere on Earth. It's completely unique, and its origin is unknown. The material is so strong that, although the Legendary Pokémon is completely hollow, its metal is indestructible. Nothing can crush it or even scratch the surface.

THE BATTLE TO PROTECT FOUR LEGENDARY POKÉMON

Ash, Brock, Dawn, Piplup, and Pikachu were visiting Frontier Brain Brandon's Battle Pyramid when a surprise visitor drove up—Maria, the local Snowpoint Temple guardian.

"Brandon, a mysterious group of people has surrounded the entrance to the temple!" Maria cried.

"Let's board the Battle Pyramid and head there right away," Brandon replied.

Eager to volunteer, Ash and his friends joined Brandon in the Battle Pyramid as it took flight. Maria began to tell them the history of her beloved Snowpoint Temple.

"Legend has it," she said, "that a long time ago, a fiery volcano erupted and swallowed Snowpoint Forest in its inferno, reducing all the rich greenery to ash. As its lava flowed downhill, it became clear its path of destruction was headed straight for Snowpoint City.

"Out of the darkness, a bright blue light shone like a beacon, bringing with it the Legendary Pokémon Regigigas. Along with Regirock, Registeel, and Regice, Regigigas stopped the ferocious volcano from destroying another step. Together, the four Legendary Pokémon saved the entire city from complete ruin!

"Then Regigigas transformed itself into a round blue stone filled with light. Inside its orb form, it fell into a deep slumber. To protect the sleeping giant, Regirock, Regice, and Registeel transformed themselves into guardian pillars made of the three basic elements of the land: rock, ice, and steel. Snowpoint Temple stands above the spot where these magical shifts took place. The Legendary Pokémon have remained there for centuries, safe and sound. Until now . . ."

As the Battle Pyramid neared the temple, Brandon spotted the source of the trouble—Hunter J, the Pokémon poacher, and her henchmen. Hunter J had set her sights on catching the Legendary Regigigas.

Before Brandon and his Battle Pyramid crew could make a move, Hunter J sent swarms of Metang and Skarmory to attack them in midair.

Whap!

Bam!

Pop!

The Battle Pyramid was trapped in a hail of a hundred slimy Sludge Bombs and fiery Flash Canons!

One of the rotors on the Battle Pyramid snapped. "Hang on, everyone!" Brandon shouted, steering into an emergency landing.

The Battle Pyramid hit the ground with a thud and slid to a slow stop. Everyone piled into Brandon's minicraft to get closer to the temple.

"They're back!" one of Hunter J's goons cried, watching the minicraft approach. "Prepare for another attack!"

Another swarm of Metang and Skarmory filled the sky, ready to strike again.

But before they could make the first move, Ash called out, "Pikachu, Thunderbolt, now!"

"Piplup, use Bubblebeam," Dawn added.

Together, their attacks cleared a path to the temple doors. Ash and his friends ran inside to the altar, where they came face-to-face with Hunter J. She proudly showed off the destruction of the temple—the rocky rubble of what once were the pillars of Regice and Regirock. With her powerful Salamence doing her bidding, J would stop at nothing to destroy the Legendary Guardians and awaken Regigigas.

"You must not go through with this," Maria pleaded. "Disturbing Regigigas could lead to disaster!"

"Pfft." Hunter J shrugged, signaling Salamence to strike again.

With a quick blast of Hyper Beam, Salamence made Registeel's pillar smash down on the path to the altar, blocking Ash and his crew from getting closer.

"All you can do now is stand and watch," Hunter J said, smirking.

Salamence fired off a series of Flamethrowers on Regigigas's blue stone.

Suddenly, a powerful red light beamed up from a triangle carving in the floor. Regigigas announced itself with an angry roar. It started firing attacks at the temple walls. The whole sacred place began to crumble.

"Regigigas, you've got to stop!" Ash warned, dodging a boulder.

But there was no reasoning with the furious giant.

"Intense rage is making it go berserk!" Maria cried.

Everyone inside the temple raced to avoid the rain of rocks falling from Regigigas's brutal blasts. Even Hunter J and Salamence were forced to retreat.

Brandon called on Regirock, Registeel, and Regice to protect the crew while they raced away. With the help of the Legendary Pokémon, the friends escaped.

Boom! The entire temple collapsed into one big pile of rocks. With a single rage-filled blast, Regigigas broke free and went on a rampage!

Brandon thought the only way to stop the Colossal Pokémon was to catch it. So he had Regirock, Registeel, and Regice launch a coordinated attack of Hyper Beam and Focus Punch. But their triple attack was no match for the massive Pokémon.

"It stopped the three of them with one hit!" Dawn exclaimed.

Brandon asked Regice to freeze Regigigas in Ice Beam. The massive Pokémon turned into an iceberg.

"You did it!" Ash cheered.

But Regigigas's rage was so strong that it crushed its ice coat into ice cubes. Regice, Registeel, and Regirock snapped back into battle action!

Hunter J swooped in on Salamence and had Ariados tie up Brandon and the crew with sticky String Shot.

"No way, Hunter J!" Ash shouted.

Suddenly, the Colossal Pokémon surprised everyone with Confuse Ray. And Regirock, Registeel, and Regice began following instructions from Regigigas! The three fired attacks at J until she was forced to retreat again.

"It's just like the legend! They've become the three pillars that protect Regigigas!" Maria exclaimed.

But the blasts continued as the four Legendary Pokémon marched away, firing in every direction, leaving a path of rocky rubble in their wake. They were heading straight for town!

"If we don't stop them, it will be a disaster!" Brock worried.

The crew was still struggling to break out of Ariados's String Shot. *"Croagunk!"* Brock's Pokémon pal shouted, bursting out of its Poké Ball.

Croagunk quickly freed its Trainer, who helped his friends get out of their sticky shackles. Then they got back in Brandon's minicraft to search for the rampaging Regigigas, Regirock, Registeel, and Regice.

They weren't the only ones looking for the Legendary Pokémon. Hunter J and her goons had set up a trap in a mountain pass. When Regigigas was in sight, Hunter J had one of her henchmen fire at the ground around its feet. Then the ship shot gobs of glue to net the Colossal Pokémon.

Regirock, Registeel, and Regice stepped up to protect Regigigas from another attack.

"Get out of my way!" Hunter J yelled, firing from her wrist cannon.

Ash and his crew arrived just in time to see Hunter J's blasts turn Registeel and Regice to stone. But before J could hit Regirock, Brandon jumped in front of her fire to protect the Legendary Pokémon. Instantly, he turned into rock, too!

"Oh no, Brandon!" Ash cried out.

Regigigas gazed down at Brandon. The Legendary Pokémon suddenly realized that Brandon and his crew had been trying to protect it.

"You meddlesome fools!" Hunter J shouted, pointing her wrist cannon at them.

When Regigigas realized its new friends were in jeopardy, it gained the strength to break free from Hunter J's glue trap. It stepped in front of Hunter J's destructive blast and protected Ash and his crew.

Sensing the tide had turned against her, Hunter J packed up her goons and hurried away.

But though the battle had ended, Brandon, Regice, and Registeel were still trapped in stone, and Ash and his pals didn't know how to free them.

"Brock, isn't there any way for us to return all of them back to normal?" Ash asked.

"I don't know . . ." Brock admitted.

"Regigigas, forgive us please!" Maria begged. "I'm sorry we weren't able to protect your slumber. But I promise, we did our best to save you. Can you save them now?"

Regigigas nodded, ready to help. It bathed the rock figures in the blue glow of Hidden Power. The stone melted away, and Registeel, Regice, and Brandon were free!

"Regigigas, are you okay?" Brandon asked.

Regigigas nodded. Whatever was left of its rage disappeared. Before the friends' eyes, Regigigas again returned to its round blue stone form.

"Regigigas's slumber will never be disturbed again!" Brandon vowed.

Brandon promised to fulfill the legend and have Regirock, Regice, and Registeel return to their rightful places as guardian pillars to protect Regigigas. As for Ash and his friends, they were happy to have helped restore both faith and the safety of the Legendary Pokémon.

LEGENDARY & MYTHICAL POKÉMON OF SINNOH

LAND FORME

GRATITUDE
POKÉMON

Height
0' 08"

Weight
4.6 LBS.

Type
GRASS

SHAYMIN

Shaymin can take on two Formes—Land and Sky. Shaymin Land Forme is shy, while Shaymin Sky Forme is spunky. But despite their personality differences, they share the same power. Shaymin can completely restore a land destroyed by pollution.

When the Gracidea flower blooms, Shaymin gains the power of flight. Wherever it goes, it clears the air of toxins and brings feelings of gratitude.

Ash and his pals once had the chance to see a Land Forme Shaymin transform into Sky Forme Shaymin. Deep in the forest, they meet Marley, a girl caring for a sick Shaymin. Ash and his crew were happy to help her restore its health. They found a field with blooming Gracidea flowers, which helped Shaymin shift into Sky Forme. The Mythical Pokémon gained wings—and the confidence to fly away on its own journey to spread Gracidea flowers across the land.

MYTHICAL POKÉMON

SKY FORME

GRATITUDE POKÉMON

Height
1' 04"

Weight
11.5 LBS.

Type
GRASS-FLYING

Grass

Electric

Ice

Fighting

Poison

Ground

Flying

Psychic

Bug

Rock

Ghost

Dragon

Dark

Steel

Fairy

Fire

Water

MYTHICAL POKÉMON

ALPHA POKÉMON

Height
10' 06"

Weight
705.5 LBS.

Type
NORMAL

ARCEUS

In the mythology of the Sinnoh region, Arceus emerged from its Egg into complete nothingness, and then shaped the world and everything in it.

For this reason, Arceus is known as the creator— and it is called the Alpha Pokémon.

MYTHICAL POKÉMON

SEA DRIFTER POKÉMON

Height
1' 04"

Weight
6.8 LBS.

Type
WATER

PHIONE

Phione gather in large groups as they drift with the current through warm seas. After floating for a time, they always return home, no matter how far they have traveled.

When the water is warm, Phione's head will inflate like a pool float, letting the Mythical Pokémon flow with the ocean's currents.

MANAPHY

From its earliest days, Manaphy possesses the power to form close bonds with any Pokémon, no matter what kind.

Manaphy is truly amazing at making friends. And its gift with emotions also extends into empathy. It can help people change their minds by showing them what it's like to be on the other side of an issue using Heart Swap.

Manaphy does not shy away from its responsibility to the community. It often acts as the leader of the Pokémon in the ocean. That's why it's called the Prince of the Sea.

MYTHICAL POKÉMON

SEAFARING POKÉMON

Height
1' 00"

Weight
3.1 LBS.

Type
WATER

LAVA DOME POKÉMON

Height
5' 07"

Weight
948.8 LBS.

Type
FIRE-STEEL

HEATRAN

Some like it hot, and Heatran is definitely that type! Said to have been born from fire, Heatran's blood boils like lava.

Heatran makes its home in caves carved out by volcanic eruptions. This Legendary Pokémon's feet can dig into rock, allowing it to walk on walls and ceilings.

DARKRAI

Darkrai defends its territory by sending intruders into a deep sleep, where they are tormented by terrible nightmares.

Darkrai definitely lives up to the "dark" in its name. According to myth, it likes to seek prey on moonless nights. It can hide easily since it's made of shadows.

MYTHICAL POKÉMON

AURORA POKÉMON

Height
4' 11"

Weight
111.3 LBS.

Type
DARK

CRESSELIA

The glimmering particles that trail from Cresselia's wings resemble a veil. This Legendary Pokémon, which brings happy dreams, is said to be a symbol of the crescent moon.

Cresselia's joy is the only thing that can balance the darkness that Darkrai brings. Ash and his friends learned firsthand just how Darkrai's grip could ruin a good night's sleep. When they visited Canalave City, they discovered all the locals had been suffering from nightmares. Darkrai typically visited the city once a year, and a Cresselia from Full Moon Island shooed it away after a one-night stay. But this year, Darkrai came early, and Cresselia was missing.

Ash and his friends volunteered to help Officer Jenny track down Cresselia. Dawn called on Swinub, who sniffed its way to a cliff where Cresselia's shrine stood. The Legendary Pokémon appeared—but so did Team Rocket. Swinub battled back the trio of villains with such passion that it evolved into Piloswine!

Once free, Cresselia headed to Canalave City to challenge Darkrai to a battle. But the Pitch-Black Pokémon was a coward. It backed down and ran out of town. Knowing the city was safe to sleep again, Cresselia bid Ash, Dawn, and their friends farewell.

LEGENDARY POKÉMON

LUNAR POKÉMON

Height
4' 11"

Weight
188.7 LBS.

Type
PSYCHIC

ALTERED FORME

GIRATINA

As punishment, the Legendary Pokémon Giratina was banished to another dimension, where everything is distorted and reversed.

This other dimension is a strange place with low gravity. Giratina is the only one who is free to travel between the Reverse World and the normal world. These two worlds are linked. When time and space

ORIGIN FORME

are damaged, the Reverse World corrects the damage. But if Giratina sees someone cause lots of damage to time and space, it will chase down the offender!

LEGENDARY POKÉMON

ALTERED FORME
RENEGADE POKÉMON

Height: 14' 09"
Weight: 1,653.5 LBS.
Type: GHOST-DRAGON

ORIGIN FORME
RENEGADE POKÉMON

Height: 22' 08"
Weight: 1,433.0 LBS.
Type: GHOST-DRAGON

LEGENDARY POKÉMON

SPATIAL POKÉMON

Height
13' 09"

Weight
740.8 LBS.

Type
WATER-DRAGON

PALKIA

It is said Palkia can cause rents and distortions in space. In ancient times, it was revered as a legend.

There are shrines to Dialga and Palkia all over Sinnoh. According to ancient legends, Palkia lives in a parallel dimension. Because it does not visit the Pokémon world often, not much is known about it. However, it is said that this Legendary Pokémon can morph and mold space.

DIALGA

It is said Dialga can control time with its mighty roar. In ancient times, it was revered as a legend.

According to legend, time began when Dialga was born. Because of its incredible relationship to every second, Dialga has complete control over clocks. The Temporal Pokémon can bend any instant to its will with its mighty Roar of Time.

LEGENDARY POKÉMON

TEMPORAL POKÉMON

Height
17' 09"

Weight
1,505.8 LBS.

Type
STEEL-DRAGON

THE LAKE

LEGENDARY POKÉMON

WILLPOWER POKÉMON

Height
1' 00"

Weight
0.7 LBS.

Type
PSYCHIC

AZELF

According to legend, Azelf brought a lasting balance to the world. It is known as "the Being of Willpower."

Legendary Pokémon Azelf, Mesprit, and Uxie were hatched from the same egg. Azelf is known for a special gift: It brought an enduring balance to the world. To keep this delicate balance without disruption, Azelf sleeps at the bottom of a lake.

GUARDIANS

MESPRIT

According to legend, Mesprit brought the first taste of joy and sorrow to people's hearts. It is known as "the Being of Emotion."

Mesprit taught people happiness, sadness, and even pain. Those emotions have added a complex and wonderful depth to life. Like Azelf, it sleeps at the bottom of a lake, but it is said that sometimes its spirit rises and flies across the lake's surface.

LEGENDARY POKÉMON

EMOTION POKÉMON

Height
1' 00"

Weight
0.7 LBS.

Type
PSYCHIC

**KNOWLEDGE
POKÉMON**

**Height
1' 00"**

**Weight
0.7 LBS.**

**Type
PSYCHIC**

UXIE

According to legend, Uxie brought the gift of intelligence to humankind. It is known as "the Being of Knowledge."

But beware: Uxie can take intelligence away, too! Legends say that if you stare into its eyes, it can wipe out your memory.

REGIGIGAS

According to legend, Regigigas built smaller models of itself out of rock, ice, and magma. It's so enormous that it could tow an entire continent behind it.

Regigigas has a connection to three Pokémon called Regirock, Registeel, and Regice. They have different types, but these Pokémon are like Regigigas in many ways. All of them have robotic voices and flashing lights on their bodies. And all are found in old and forgotten places.

COLOSSAL POKÉMON

Height
12' 02"

Weight
925.9 LBS.

Type
NORMAL

LEGENDARY & MYTHICAL POKÉMON OF UNOVA

THE SWORDS OF

LEGENDARY POKÉMON

IRON WILL POKÉMON

Height
6' 11"

Weight
551.2 LBS.

Type
STEEL-
FIGHTING

COBALION

Like its body, Cobalion's heart is tough as steel. Legends say that in the past, it protected Pokémon from harmful people.

Cobalion's glare is even tougher than its body. With one look, Cobalion can get even the most out-of-control Pokémon to settle down. It cannot stand rudeness or disrespect. So it will remind any Pokémon—or any person, for that matter—to mind its manners. In fact, according to ancient tales, Cobalion has been known to protect Pokémon from human bullies.

JUSTICE

VIRIZION

According to legend, Virizion can move so swiftly that its opponents are left bewildered. Its horns are lovely and graceful—and as sharp as blades.

You just might miss this Legendary Pokémon as it whizzes past you! Watching Virizion move is like trying to follow the wind. If the Grassland Pokémon chooses to stay in one place, it can mow a foe down with its horns.

LEGENDARY POKÉMON

GRASSLAND POKÉMON

Height
6' 07"

Weight
440.9 LBS.

Type
GRASS-FIGHTING

LEGENDARY POKÉMON

CAVERN POKÉMON

Height
6' 03"

Weight
573.2 LBS.

Type
ROCK-
FIGHTING

TERRAKION

Legends tell of a time when Terrakion attacked a mighty castle to protect its Pokémon friends. They say it knocked down a giant wall with the force of its charge.

Although it might look like it's all brawn, Terrakion actually has a big heart. It has a soft spot for any Pokémon in need. When a human war forced a group of Pokémon from their peaceful homes, Terrakion stepped in to save them.

RESOLUTE FORME

NORMAL FORME

KELDEO

Keldeo travels the world visiting beaches and riverbanks, where it can race across the water. When this Mythical Pokémon is filled with resolve, it gains a blinding speed.

The Colt Pokémon is so swift that it's actually hard to see. When it's determined, its body fills with a strong power that increases its speed. Its great leaps become impossible to follow with the naked eye.

MYTHICAL POKÉMON

COLT POKÉMON

Height
4' 07"

Weight
106.9 LBS.

Type
WATER-FIGHTING

MYTHICAL POKÉMON

PALEOZOIC POKÉMON

Height
4' 11"

Weight
181.9 LBS.

Type
BUG-STEEL

GENESECT

The powerful cannon on Genesect's back is the result of Team Plasma's meddling. This Mythical Pokémon is 300 million years old.

The ancient bug Pokémon was just a fossil . . . until evil Team Plasma got their hands on it. They brought Genesect back to life, and they also changed it forever.

VICTINI

According to myth, Victini can bring victory in any kind of competition. Because it creates unlimited energy, it can share the overflow with others.

This little powerhouse has so much pep to share that it can completely recharge another person or Pokémon. With Victini on your side, you can't lose.

INCARNATE FORME

THERIAN FORME

LEGENDARY POKÉMON

INCARNATE FORME

BOLT STRIKE POKÉMON

Height: 4' 11"

Weight: 134.5 LBS.

Type: ELECTRIC-FLYING

THERIAN FORME

BOLT STRIKE POKÉMON

Height: 9' 10"

Weight: 134.5 LBS.

Type: ELECTRIC-FLYING

THUNDURUS

Thundurus can discharge powerful electric bolts from the spikes on its tail. This Pokémon causes terrible lightning storms, which often result in forest fires.

This Legendary Pokémon has started some pretty legendary blazes. So be sure to look out for fierce lightning if you're below this prickly Pokémon.

INCARNATE FORME

THERIAN FORME

TORNADUS

Wrapped in its cloud, Tornadus flies at 200 miles per hour. This Legendary Pokémon causes fierce windstorms with gales that can knock down houses.

While Tornadus might blow by in an instant, its power over air can create lasting damage. With the tap of its tail, Tornadus can cover the land with a wild wind. With a little release of energy, it can create a big storm. With a whistle, Tornadus can blow a breeze so tough it will topple the buildings below.

LEGENDARY POKÉMON

INCARNATE FORME

CYCLONE POKÉMON

Height: 4' 11"
Weight: 138.9 LBS.
Type: FLYING

THERIAN FORME

CYCLONE POKÉMON

Height: 4' 07"
Weight: 138.9 LBS.
Type: FLYING

71

INCARNATE FORME

THERIAN FORME

LEGENDARY POKÉMON

INCARNATE FORME

ABUNDANCE POKÉMON

Height: 4' 11"

Weight: 134.5 LBS.

Type: GROUND-FLYING

THERIAN FORME

ABUNDANCE POKÉMON

Height: 4' 03"

Weight: 149.9 LBS.

Type: GROUND-FLYING

LANDORUS

Because its arrival helps crops grow, Landorus is welcomed as "the Guardian of the Fields." This Legendary Pokémon uses the energy of wind and lightning to enrich the soil.

Although Landorus soars in the sky, it has an incredible power over the land. No matter where the plot of dirt or what its condition, Landorus can transform it into an incredible spot for crops with its arrival. Using its tail, it will greatly fertilize any field and help it yield a beautiful bounty. The crop will grow taller than any planted by hand, and it will rise up almost instantly.

THE RAGE AND REVIVAL OF LEGENDS

Ash and his friends Iris and Cilan were visiting Milos Island in search of Revival Herbs needed to restore injured Pokémon to health. But when they arrived, their guide, Lewis, informed them that all the Revival Herbs he could find were dried out—and his Pokémon were getting sick! There was one Revival Herb left in his stock.

Lewis was determined to bring the land back to life. He planned to lead a special Rainmaking Ceremony with his Pokémon, Gothorita, the next day. Ash, Iris, and Cilan eagerly agreed to take part.

So Lewis began to tell them the legend of Milos Island...

Long ago, Thundurus and Tornadus were locked in an epic battle. Landorus bravely stepped in to stop their fighting and was horribly wounded. The ancient people of Milos Island used Revival Herbs to

help the Legendary Pokémon recover. It regained its strength and was able to break up the battle. To thank the people who had healed it, Landorus turned Milos Island into a paradise full of Revival Herbs.

The next morning, the kids headed to the Shrine of Landorus, a big stone pillar covered in ancient carvings.

"Landorus!" Lewis called out. "The Revival Herbs have all dried up. We ask for rain for Milos Island!"

Lewis's Gothorita echoed his words with a song. Its voice created a pink glow that traveled up into the clouds.

Suddenly, a giant dark cloud took form. At first it looked like rain, but then a strange shape appeared in the sky. Out of the clouds emerged the Legendary Pokémon Tornadus! It sent back-to-back attacks of Hurricane and Air Slash.

"Look out!" Iris warned. "Why is Tornadus so angry?"

"Something happened to Tornadus's stone-pillar home," Lewis replied.

Ash, Lewis, and Iris hurried away to investigate. Soon they found Tornadus's stone had been smashed! Now there was nothing to stop the rage of the Cyclone Pokémon.

"Who could have done such a thing?" Lewis wondered.

Worse yet, the friends discovered Thundurus's stone pillar had also been smashed. There were two angry Legendary Pokémon on the loose!

"*Thuuuundurus!*" Thundurus shouted.

"*Torrrrrnaaaaadus!*" Tornadus yelled back.

The two began to fight each other, just like in the Legend of Milos Island.

"The battle between Tornadus and Thundurus is starting all over again!" Lewis realized.

"We've got to stop those two, and fast!" Ash declared.

Snivy shot Leaf Storm. *Pew, pew, pew!*

Excadrill fired Focus Blast. *Wham!*

Axew drummed up Dragon Rage. *Boom!*

Stunfisk released Mud Bomb. *Slap!*

But the Legendary Pokémon easily dodged their attacks. So Lewis asked Gothorita to try reasoning with them.

 Gothorita sang the message with all its might, but it only made the Pokémon angrier. Tornadus's wind knocked down trees in the forest. Thundurus's bolts broke rocks right off the mountainside. The Legendary Pokémon were intent on destroying each other, and in the process, they would also destroy Milos Island!

"There's only one thing left to do," Lewis said. "We have to have a Shrine Maiden summon the guardian of Milos Island, Landorus."

"Where are we going to find a Shrine Maiden?" Iris asked.

"Iris, I'm looking right at her!" Lewis replied, smiling.

Once she dressed in traditional Milos Island garb, Iris was ready to give it her all! Lewis came prepared with mysterious stones that increased Gothorita's power.

When they reached the pillar of Landorus, Iris bowed her head. "Landorus, I beg for your help from the bottom of my heart."

Bathed in a pink glow, Gothorita sang her feelings to the shrine. A powerful yellow light shined over the area, and then shot straight up into the sky. The light was absorbed into a figure—Landorus!

"Landorus," Lewis addressed the Legendary Pokémon with respect. "Tornadus and Thundurus are battling so fiercely, they're going to destroy Milos Island! I beg you to stop them!"

"Landor!" It nodded, ready to take action.

A bolt of lightning burst through the gray sky, and Landorus followed it to find Tornadus and Thundurus. Landorus pleaded with them to stop their petty fighting.

"Thundurus!" the Pokémon replied with a roar, firing Focus Blast.

"Torrrrrrnadus!" the other snarled back, shooting Hurricane.

Landorus had convinced Tornadus and Thundurus to stop fighting each other. Instead, they joined forces to attack it!

"It's two against one!" Ash yelped.

Landorus defended itself with a powerful burst of Extrasensory. Tornadus hit back with Hammer Arm, slamming Landorus into a mountainside. Landorus was trapped and under attack as Thundurus threw Focus Blast!

Suddenly, Landorus broke free and launched Hyper Beam. But when Tornadus responded with Hidden Power, big rocks were blasted off the mountainside.

Crash!

"Landorus, behind you!" Lewis cried.

Gothorita jumped in and fired Psyshock to stop Thundurus from its sneak attack.

"*Laaaaaaandoruuuuuuuus!*" Landorus shouted, sending a burst of Hyper Beam.

Direct hit! While Thundurus and Tornadus tried to recover from the wallop, Landorus again tried to reason with them.

Suddenly, laser lines surrounded the three Legendary Pokémon! The lasers formed a cube cage, locking up the trio.

"*Thunduuuuur!*" Thundurus cried, trying to blast its way out.

But even these powerful Legendary Pokémon couldn't break the bonds of their laser cages.

"Who did that?!" Lewis asked.

"Who? That is the question, indeed," replied James. It was Team Rocket!

"So you're the ones who destroyed the stone shrines!" Lewis said.

"Aren't you smart?!" James said. "And we knew when they arrived, you'd have to summon Landorus."

"Now they all belong to us!" Jessie rejoiced.

"Not as long as we're here," Ash replied.

Together, he and Iris and Lewis and Cilan directed their Pokémon to attack.

Roggenrola fired Flash Cannon at the cages. *Whap!*

Emolga threw Hidden Power. *Pow!*

Pansage blasted Solar Beam. *Boom!*

Gothorita added Shadow Ball. *Swish!*

But when the smoke cleared, the three Legendary Pokémon were still in their cages.

Team Rocket hopped in a helicopter and loaded up the three cages.

"Finders keepers, losers weepers," James said, waving good-bye.

"Weep, losers!" Meowth chuckled as the helicopter took off.

But Ash, Iris, Cilan, and Lewis refused give up. They banded together and fired at the helicopter instead of the cages.

So Roggenrola fired Flash Cannon. *Whap!*

Emolga threw Hidden Power. *Pow!*

Pansage blasted Solar Beam. *Boom!*

It worked! The helicopter began to smoke, and Team Rocket had to release the cages from the helicopter.

The three cages fell from the sky, landing in the valley.

"Laaaandorus!" Landorus cried, wincing in pain.

Landorus was injured. It was in no shape to continue fighting, but Tornadus and Thundurus started to attack it again!

Only one thing could save Landorus—the very last Revival Herb.

"Gothorita, send the Revival Herb to Landorus!" Lewis instructed.

Gothorita began to sing again as it used its powerful pink glow to carry the Revival Herb across the valley to Landorus.

Thundurus and Tornadus launched a coordinated attack to stop it from reaching Landorus.

"Landorus!" it shouted, firing Protect. It received the Revival Herb!

With its strength restored, Landorus rose back into the sky.

"It's happening exactly like the Milos Island legend!" Cilan exclaimed.

Powerful Landorus finished off Thundurus and Tornadus with a burst of Hyper Beam! Then it again tried to reason with them. With one hand on each of their hearts, Landorus conveyed its hope to restore peace to Milos Island. Gothorita added her song to his plea.

"It looks like Landorus finally got through to them!" Ash said.

The dark clouds cleared, and the sun once again shone down on Milos Island. But in the light, Lewis could see the damage the battle had inflicted on the land.

"Landorus, please, heal this island!" Lewis implored. "Return it to its beautiful state so the Revival Herbs can grow again!"

"Landorus!" it promised.

But Landorus couldn't do it all on its own. It needed its legendary brothers Thundurus and Tornadus to restore the delicate balance.

Thundurus brought its power over rain. Tornadus added its power over wind. Landorus brought the Revival Herb seeds. They instantly sprouted up again across the island.

"Wow!" Lewis cried in awe. "Landorus, Tornadus, and Thundurus, thank you!"

"Thank you!" Ash, Iris, and Cilan echoed.

Lewis vowed to continue to take care of Milos Island. As they said good-bye to their new friend, Ash, Iris, and Cilan knew they were leaving it in good hands.

THE LEGENDARY

LEGENDARY POKÉMON

ZEKROM

DEEP BLACK POKÉMON

Height
9' 06"

Weight
760.6 LBS.

Type
DRAGON-
FLYING

Legends say Zekrom helps those who pursue their ideals. It surrounds itself with thunderclouds to travel unseen, and its tail can generate electricity.

Zekrom travels under the cover of dark clouds. It can fire lightning from the electricity in its tail. So, during a storm, you might wonder—is that weather, or is that the Deep Black Pokémon?

Professor Juniper once questioned whether Zekrom was responsible for taking her computer system offline. But even if it gets in tangles with technology, rest assured, Zekrom only has the best of intentions. It will always be there to help anyone who pursues his or her ideals.

UNOVA TRIO

RESHIRAM

Legends say Reshiram is drawn to those who value the truth. The flare of its fiery tail can disrupt the atmosphere and cause strange weather patterns.

Reshiram might look like snow, but it's actually burning hot. In fact, it's white-hot! This Pokémon can start a fierce fire. Reshiram will not hesitate to use its incredible powers to protect those who want to build a world of truth.

LEGENDARY POKÉMON

VAST WHITE POKÉMON

Height
10' 06"

Weight
6,727.5 LBS.

Type
DRAGON-FIRE

LEGENDARY POKÉMON

BOUNDARY POKÉMON

Height: 9' 10"
Weight: 716.5 LBS.
Type: DRAGON-ICE

KYUREM

When the freezing energy inside Kyurem leaked out, its entire body froze. Legends say it will become whole with the help of a hero who will bring truth or ideals.

Kyurem itself is never full of hot air—either in its temperatures or lies. Inside its body, this Legendary Pokémon has an icy energy that can freeze out its foes. However, because it can easily spring a leak, Kyurem has accidentally frozen itself over.

LEGENDARY POKÉMON

BLACK KYUREM

BOUNDARY POKÉMON

Height: *10' 10"*
Weight: *716.5 LBS.*
Type: *DRAGON-ICE*

BLACK KYUREM

LEGENDARY POKÉMON

WHITE KYUREM

BOUNDARY POKÉMON

Height: *11' 10"*
Weight: *716.5 LBS.*
Type: *DRAGON-ICE*

WHITE KYUREM

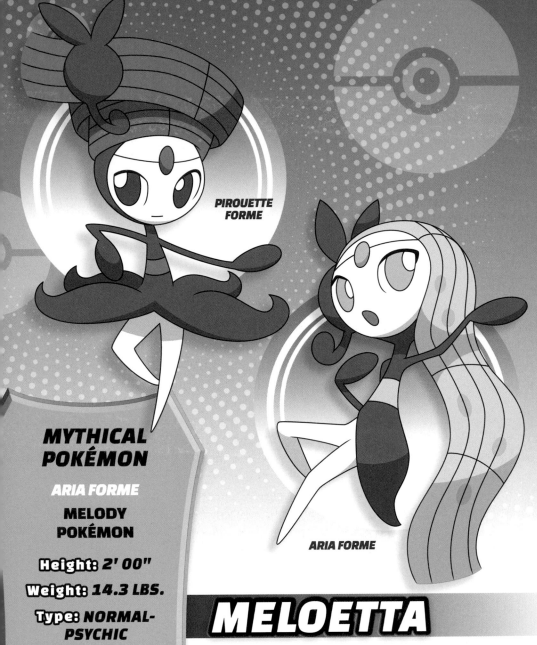

PIROUETTE
FORME

ARIA FORME

MYTHICAL POKÉMON

ARIA FORME

MELODY POKÉMON

Height: 2' 00"

Weight: 14.3 LBS.

Type: NORMAL-PSYCHIC

PIROUETTE FORME

MELODY POKÉMON

Height: 2' 00"

Weight: 14.3 LBS.

Type: NORMAL-FIGHTING

MELOETTA

When Meloetta sings, its voice can control the emotions of people or Pokémon. The beautiful melodies of this Mythical Pokémon can bring aching sadness or radiant joy.

Behind Meloetta's sweet sounds is incredible power. Meloetta literally puts emotion in its songs. It can transform the mood of anyone who hears its melodies.

MELOETTA & ASH: THE EVOLUTION OF FRIENDSHIP

Ash has a special bond with the Melody Pokémon. Whenever it's in trouble, Ash is there to save the day! But their bond goes both ways. Whenever Ash is in trouble, Meloetta appears. Here's how their friendship evolved . . .

Ash first met Meloetta at Pokéstar Studios in Virbank City. He saved Meloetta from a falling piece of the studio's set. Ash is always ready to help a Pokémon in need, so he didn't think much of the moment. But Meloetta turned into a fan who secretly started following him on his journey.

When Team Rocket saw an opportunity to steal Meloetta, they tossed their electric net. Meloetta escaped, but it rolled down a huge hill and landed in the middle of the road. Luckily, Ash and his friends were just driving by in Cynthia's truck. They immediately stopped and saved the Mythical Pokémon. Using Cynthia's medicine, Ash nursed Meloetta back to health. It flew away, but that wasn't the last Ash and his friends would see or hear of the Melody Pokémon.

Meloetta's voice has a mysteriously powerful strength. When Onix chased after Ash and his friends, they couldn't seem to battle it back. So the Mythical Pokémon began to sing. Upon hearing Meloetta's incredible voice, another brave Onix was so deeply moved that it rose and stopped the other Onix from attacking.

Although Meloetta is terribly timid, it wouldn't miss the chance to root for Ash in the Junior Cup! But even when Ash wasn't competing, Meloetta was always watching over Ash and his friends. Meloetta helped him find shelter and food in the rain. Meloetta also aided Ash across a broken bridge. The Melody Pokémon is as sweet as its song.

LEGENDARY & MYTHICAL POKÉMON OF KALOS

VOLCANION

Since Fire-type Pokémon are generally weak against Water-type Pokémon, it might seem strange to have a Pokémon that's both. But make no mistake, Volcanion is a powerhouse because of that very combination. When the fire heats up water, it turns into steam—and Volcanion can shoot a blast of steam so strong that it can move a mountain.

Despite its strength, Volcanion prefers to stay out of sight. This Mythical Pokémon lives in the mountains and stays far away from humans. The arms on its back can shoot out steam with incredibly destructive force, though it often uses these steam clouds to cover its escape. It likes to disappear under a cloak of vapor if it encounters trouble, instead of attacking.

MYTHICAL POKÉMON

STEAM POKÉMON

Height
5' 07"

Weight
429.9 LBS.

Type
FIRE-WATER

LEGENDARY POKÉMON

LIFE POKÉMON

Height
9' 10"

Weight
474.0 LBS.

Type
FAIRY

XERNEAS

Xerneas's horns shine in all the colors of the rainbow. It is said that this Legendary Pokémon can share the gift of endless life.

Before Xerneas was reborn, it took the shape of a tree and slept for a whole millennium. After a thousand years of beauty sleep, it's no wonder Xerneas is so special.

YVELTAL

When Yveltal spreads its dark wings, its feathers give off a red glow. It is said that this Legendary Pokémon can absorb the life energy of others.

The crimson light underneath those wings is beautiful to behold, but beware—it might just get ahold of you!

ZYGARDE 10%

ZYGARDE 50%

ZYGARDE COMPLETE

LEGENDARY POKÉMON

ORDER POKÉMON

ZYGARDE 50%

Height: 16' 05"

Weight: 672.4 LBS.

Type: DRAGON-GROUND

ZYGARDE 10%

Height: 3' 11"

Weight: 73.9 LBS.

Type: DRAGON-GROUND

ZYGARDE COMPLETE

Height: 14' 09"

Weight: 1,344.8 LBS.

Type: DRAGON-GROUND

ZYGARDE

Zygarde dwells deep within a cave in the Kalos region. It is said that this Legendary Pokémon is a guardian of the ecosystem.

Zygarde prefers to stay out of sight, but it will appear if the delicate balance of the ecosystem is in trouble.

HOOPA CONFINED

HOOPA UNBOUND

HOOPA

Hoopa is heralded as having a huge amount of power. If only it would use it for good instead of greed!

Hoopa's taste for riches knows no bounds. And with the strength of a Mythical Pokémon, it has the luxury of being able to take what it desires. Hoopa once wanted a royal treasure so badly, it stole the entire castle. Can you imagine carrying a big brick building just to get a few baubles?

MYTHICAL POKÉMON

HOOPA CONFINED

MISCHIEF POKÉMON

Height: 1' 08"

Weight: 19.8 LBS.

Type: PSYCHIC-GHOST

HOOPA UNBOUND

DJINN POKÉMON

Height: 21' 04"

Weight: 1,080.3 LBS.

Type: PSYCHIC-DARK

DIANCIE   MEGA DIANCIE

MYTHICAL POKÉMON

JEWEL POKÉMON

Height
2'04"

Weight
19.14 LBS.

Type
ROCK-FAIRY

DIANCIE

Perhaps Diancie should also be measured in carats, because it is known as the Jewel Pokémon. This Mythical Pokémon is truly dazzling. It shimmers and shines just like a precious stone. This stunning, sparkling pink Pokémon wows anyone lucky enough to catch a glimpse of it.

According to myth, when Carbink suddenly transforms into Diancie, its dazzling appearance is the most beautiful sight in existence. It has the power to compress carbon from the atmosphere, forming diamonds between its hands.

MYTHICAL POKÉMON

MEGA DIANCIE

JEWEL POKÉMON

Height: *3' 07"*
Weight: *61.3 LBS.*
Type: *ROCK-FAIRY*

LEGENDARY & MYTHICAL POKÉMON OF ALOLA

ARTIFICIAL
POKÉMON

Height
3' 03"

Weight
177.5 LBS.

Type
STEEL-FAIRY

MAGEARNA

Magearna was built many centuries ago by human inventors. The rest of this Pokémon's mechanical body is just a vehicle for its true self: the Soul-Heart contained in its chest. This incredible technological advancement is known as the Artificial Pokémon.

Although Magearna might be a machine, it is a highly functional and powerful robot Pokémon, and is very sensitive. When humans speak, it understands. It can also feel other Pokémon's emotions and even discern their thoughts. If a Pokémon is hurting or in trouble, Magearna will come to its rescue! This Mythical Pokémon can't stand to see someone suffer.

Its Soul-Heart is created by humans and made of life energy from Pokémon. It is the most vital part of Magearna's entire body and appears as a glowing orb in its chest.

When Magearna sleeps, it folds itself up into a sphere that resembles a Poké Ball. It is also known to curl up into this shape when it is sad.

LEGENDARY POKÉMON

NEBULA POKÉMON

Height
0' 08"

Weight
0.02 LBS.

Type
PSYCHIC

COSMOG

This mysterious Legendary Pokémon is one of Alola's best-kept secrets. According to legend, there was a time when the only people who knew of Cosmog's existence were the kings of Alola. Now the Aether Foundation, a famous Pokémon health institute in the region, has devoted resources to learning more about this unique and relatively unknown Pokémon.

What we do know is Cosmog is not shy. Fearless and curious, Cosmog is always looking to make new friends. If you show this Legendary Pokémon kindness, it will immediately treat you like a pal. Unfortunately, because of its trusting nature, Cosmog can often fall into dangerous situations.

Cosmog reportedly came to the Alola region from another world, but its origins are shrouded in mystery. Known as the child of the stars, it grows by gathering dust from the atmosphere. It is now also known as the Nebula Pokémon. When bathed in light, Cosmog's body can absorb the glow, and grow. It can also become larger by gathering the atmospheric dust. But no matter how big it gets, Cosmog is still lightweight because its body is made of gas, so it goes anywhere the wind blows.

COSMOG   **COSMOEM**

SOLGALEO   **LUNALA**

COSMOEM

Don't underestimate this Pokémon because of its small size. The Legendary Pokémon Cosmoem weighs in at over a ton! It is unknown why it is quite so heavy, and its core is gathering a mass of an unidentified substance.

Cosmoem never moves, radiating a gentle warmth as it develops inside the hard shell that surrounds it. Long ago, people referred to it as the cocoon of the stars, and some still think its origins lie in another world.

If you ever see Cosmoem, you might wonder whether it is alive, because it stays completely still at all times. But it lets off heat from the center of its body, so if you get the chance to touch the Protostar Pokémon, it will feel warm.

LEGENDARY POKÉMON

PROTOSTAR POKÉMON

Height
0' 04"

Weight
2,204.4 LBS.

Type
PSYCHIC

COSMOG   COSMOEM

SOLGALEO   LUNALA

LEGENDARY POKÉMON

SUNNE POKÉMON

Height
11' 02"

Weight
507.1 LBS.

Type
PSYCHIC-STEEL

SOLGALEO

Solgaleo's entire body radiates a bright light that can wipe away the darkness of night. This Legendary Pokémon apparently makes its home in another world, and it returns there when its third eye becomes active.

When Solgaleo appears in the Pokémon world, it bears a striking resemblance to the sun, particularly in its starlike mane. And because of its radiant power, everyone from ancient times to today considers Solgaleo to be the ambassador of the sun. It is also known as the beast that devours the sun. Solgaleo is thought to be the male evolved form of Cosmog.

COSMOG

COSMOEM

SOLGALEO

LUNALA

MOONE
POKÉMON

Height
13' 01"

Weight
264.6 LBS.

Type
PSYCHIC-
GHOST

LUNALA

Lunala's wide wings soak up the light, plunging the brightest day into shadow. This Legendary Pokémon apparently makes its home in another world, and it returns there when its third eye becomes active.

When it opens its golden-crescent-tipped wings, it looks just like a starry night. This revered Pokémon's wings aren't just a substitute for the evening sky—they can turn the sky's light into energy. Lunala is known as the messenger of the moon. Since ancient times, it has also been known as the beast who calls the moon. Lunala is thought to be the female evolved form of Cosmog.

COSMOG

COSMOEM

SOLGALEO

LUNALA

PRISM
POKÉMON

Height
7' 10"

Weight
507.1 LBS.

Type
PSYCHIC

NECROZMA

Some think Necrozma arrived from another world many eons ago. When it emerges from its underground slumber, it seems to absorb light for use as energy to power its laser-like blasts. It can even sap energy from a foe.

You definitely don't want to wake up this Legendary Pokémon if you can help it! So don't go around stomping your feet, because nasty Necrozma hibernates underground. And once the

DUSK MANE NECROZMA

DAWN WINGS NECROZMA

ULTRA NECROZMA

LEGENDARY POKÉMON

DUSK MANE NECROZMA
Height: 12' 06"

Weight: 1,104.1 LBS.

Type: PSYCHIC-STEEL

DAWN WINGS NECROZMA
Height: 13' 09"

Weight: 771.6 LBS.

Type: PSYCHIC-GHOST

ULTRA NECROZMA
Height: 24' 07"

Weight: 507.1 LBS.

Type: PSYCHIC-DRAGON

ferocious Prism Pokémon wakes up, it will not cease furiously firing laser beams from its arms. They can blast through anything and everything!

This savage Pokémon gets even angrier when it feels drained, and it will appear to be in pain. But don't mistake its weakness for vulnerability—Necrozma is always a vicious opponent.

MYTHICAL POKÉMON

GLOOMDWELLER POKÉMON

Height
2' 04"

Weight
48.9 LBS.

Type
FIGHTING-GHOST

MARSHADOW

Very few people have seen Marshadow, so it was considered a rumor. Always cowering in the shadows, it watches others closely and mimics their movements. Marshadow has the remarkable ability to perfectly imitate other Pokémon and their precise movements and force. Marshadow really gets into character performing its flawless impressions and can grow even more powerful than the Pokémon it is pretending to be.

ZENITH MARSHADOW

This Legendary Pokémon is the first known Pokémon in existence to be both a Fighting-type and Ghost-type Pokémon. Since Psychic types are weak against Ghost types, this gives Marshadow an awesome advantage.

Although it is a talented impressionist, Marshadow does not like the spotlight and is afraid to be revealed. It stays carefully hidden, where it can observe but not be seen. It is rare for a fellow Pokémon to catch a glimpse of this shy, sly Pokémon, and even rarer for a human to spot it.

LEGENDARY POKÉMON

LAND SPIRIT POKÉMON

Height
6' 03"

Weight
100.3 LBS.

Type
GRASS-FAIRY

TAPU BULU

Tapu Bulu has a reputation for laziness—rather than battling directly, it commands vines to pin down its foes. The plants that grow abundantly in its wake give it energy. It's known as the guardian of Ula'ula Island.

Tapu Bulu not only makes plants grow, but uses their energy to gain strength. It is so strong, it can uproot giant trees and swing them in the air. According to myth, it once used this twirling tree technique to rid its valuable ruins of thieves.

You might say that this Legendary Pokémon works smart instead of hard to fight its enemies. Once Tapu Bulu traps its opponent with vines, it finishes the battle by tackling with its tough horns. And it can even make its own wooden horns grow with its amazing plant power.

Although Tapu Bulu is a formidable foe, it prefers not to fight. It is also concerned that its very appearance will scare other Pokémon. So, you might just hear Tapu Bulu before you see it. It sings a loud ring to let everyone know that it's close by. Follow that chime if you want to set your eyes on the amazing Tapu Bulu!

TAPU FINI

Tapu Fini can control and cleanse water, washing away impurities. When threatened, it summons a dense fog to confuse its enemies. This Pokémon draws energy from ocean currents. It's known as the guardian of Poni Island.

Tapu Fini does not like to battle, because it fears getting hurt, but its ability to create disorienting fog keeps it out of the fray.

But Tapu Fini doesn't just use water for its own protection—it also protects the water. The water it purifies can clean anything—even the mind. And so many seek out Tapu Fini's water, but not all have the purest of intentions. So, as a test, Tapu Fini sees whether they can stand up to its strong steam. However, even getting the chance to be blasted with this Legendary Pokémon's fog is lucky. It doesn't like to present itself to people, because it has been faced with too many scoundrels. Tapu Fini never shows emotion, even during battle.

LEGENDARY POKÉMON

LAND SPIRIT POKÉMON

Height
4' 03"

Weight
46.7 LBS.

Type
WATER-FAIRY

TAPU KOKO

Somewhat lacking in attention span, Tapu Koko is quick to anger but just as quickly forgets why it's angry. Calling thunderclouds lets it store up lightning as energy. It's known as the guardian of Melemele Island.

Tapu Koko is electrifying on the battlefield! After it stockpiles lightning from storm clouds in its body, it can strike in a flash when it comes face-to-face with a foe. This Legendary Pokémon attacks with such speed, an opponent can't even see it coming—Tapu Koko is too quick to be spotted with the naked eye.

This curious and playful Pokémon often takes an interest in other Pokémon and people. It took a shine to Ash when he arrived in Alola. First, Tapu Koko snatched Ash's hat. Then it challenged him to a battle and even made sure Ash was given a Z-Ring and Electrium Z.

LEGENDARY POKÉMON

LAND SPIRIT POKÉMON

Height
5' 11"

Weight
45.2 LBS.

Type
ELECTRIC-FAIRY

**LAND SPIRIT
POKÉMON**

Height
3' 11"

Weight
41.0 LBS.

Type
PSYCHIC-
FAIRY

TAPU LELE

As Tapu Lele flutters through the air, people in search of good health gather up the glowing scales that fall from its body. It draws energy from the scent of flowers. It's known as the guardian of Akala Island.

Though Tapu Lele can gain power through its nose, if it doesn't feel energized enough for battle, it will use a clever strategy with status conditions to stop an enemy.

However, it is known more for its healing talents than its fighting skills. According to an old Alolan myth, Tapu Lele brought peace to the warring Alolan Islands by sharing its special scales to restore the health of the warriors. More recently, our hero Ash was healed from some scratches he got while rescuing Wimpod by a sprinkle of Tapu Lele's shiny scales.

But too much of a good thing can become harmful. Touching too many of Tapu Lele's medicinal scales can cause damage—a fact that it is aware of and often uses deliberately. And you won't find this Pokémon cautioning someone if they're in the danger zone, so look out!

ZERAORA

Zeraora is known for its supercharged claws that pack a powerful punch. It electrifies its claws and tears its opponents apart with them. Even if they dodge its attack, they'll be electrocuted by the flying sparks.

In fact, it can build a massive ball of electric shocks with Plasma Fists. The blast is so electrifying that a Trainer and former Ultra Ranger named Dia called on Zeraora to use Plasma Fists to ward off the terrifying Ultra Beast Guzzlord. And it's no wonder that when Ash and Pikachu were lucky enough to battle the Mythical Zeraora, it was Plasma Fists that finished that match, too.

MYTHICAL POKÉMON

THUNDERCLAP POKÉMON

Height
4' 11"

Weight
98.1 LBS.

Type
ELECTRIC

In addition to power, Zeraora also has speed on its side. During a battle, Zeraora's Electric-type attacks are fast as lightning! And while most opponents will focus on its sharp claws, a wise Trainer will be careful of its tail, too. It might look soft, but if you pet it, it will zap you.

TYPE: NULL

LAND SPIRIT POKÉMON

Height
6' 03"

Weight
265.7 LBS.

Type
NORMAL

The synthetic Pokémon known as Type: Null wears a heavy mask to keep its power in check. Some fear that without the mask, it would lose control of its powers and go on a destructive rampage.

Type: Null was manufactured, and is a force to be reckoned with. This Legendary Pokémon possesses a mysterious hidden strength that can cause incredible damage, and must be restrained. Many fear Type: Null's fury, so its control mask limits its capabilities.

TYPE: NULL IS ALSO FOUND IN THE GALAR REGION.

TYPE: NULL   **SILVALLY**

TYPE: NULL

SILVALLY

SILVALLY

Silvally evolves from Type: Null. Learning to trust its Trainer caused this Pokémon to evolve and discard the mask that kept its power tightly controlled. Silvally can change its type in battle, making it a formidable opponent.

Silvally's ability to shift its type can really surprise its enemies. If you begin a battle with the Normal-type Pokémon, you don't really know what kind of foe you'll face. Just know that this Synthetic Pokémon is a force to be reckoned with—in any place, time, or type.

LEGENDARY POKÉMON

SYNTHETIC POKÉMON

Height
7' 07"

Weight
221.6 LBS.

Type
NORMAL

MISSION: TOTAL RECALL

Alone in her room, Ash's friend Lillie was crying. Something she'd seen had brought back a terrifying memory that she couldn't stop thinking about: a Pokémon with sharp claws jumping at her. She didn't remember what happened, or even when—she could just see the Pokémon's fiery red eyes. It left her afraid to touch any Pokémon, even her best buddy, Snowy, the little Alolan Vulpix.

Snowy wagged its tails, looking up at her with its big blue eyes. But Lillie just couldn't muster the courage to hold it.

"I'm so sorry," she whispered with tears in her eyes.

When Lillie's brother, Gladion, returned to his room that night, he was surprised to see the wicked scientist Faba waiting there for him. Faba worked for Gladion's mother, Lusamine, who was the head of a research lab in Alola called the Aether Foundation. Faba had created the Legendary Pokémon Silvally to battle Ultra Beasts and be part of his evil experiments. Then, to restrain its power, Faba had put a horrible helmet on it, making it take on a new name—Type: Null. Gladion did not like the way Type: Null was being treated by Faba, so he rescued it and had been secretly caring for it ever since.

"What do you want?" Gladion barked at Faba.

"I came here to retrieve Type: Null," Faba told Gladion, adding that it was an order from Gladion's mother.

"You think I would give Silvally back to you?!" Gladion replied.

Gladion called on his Lycanroc and Umbreon to battle back Faba's Alakazam and Hypno. Lycanroc threw a sharp Stone Edge, but Hypno shattered it with Reflect. Umbreon sent a dark Shadow Ball, but Alakazam used Miracle Eye light to destroy it. Before Gladion could strike again, Faba had Hypno use Hypnosis to knock out Lycanroc.

Then Alakazam slammed Umbreon against the wall with a bold Psychic. The only one left standing was Gladion.

"Give up!" Faba told him.

"Never!" Gladion cried.

"Hypno, use Hypnosis," Faba commanded. Then he turned to Gladion. "This is the perfect time for you to take a nap."

In a daze, Gladion called out for Silvally, but he was soon fast asleep. Faba nabbed the Legendary Pokémon and slipped out.

At school the next day, Lillie's classmates and teachers were trying to cheer her up. With their support, she decided to muster her courage and see if she could touch Snowy . . . but when Snowy leaped over, she instantly got scared and didn't hug it. She was sad, but she promised her Pokémon she wouldn't give up trying.

At the end of the day, Ash, Rotom, Pikachu, and their Legendary Cosmog pal, Nebby, offered to walk Lillie and Snowy home. As they strolled, they talked about Lillie's fear of touching Pokémon and her scary flashback. She wished she could remember everything that had happened, not just the part where the terrifying Pokémon jumped at her. She thought that recalling the full story might be the key to unlocking her fear.

"How could I have forgotten such an awful thing?" she wondered. "I've got to know every detail."

Psychic-type Nebby decided to use Teleport to help Lillie. First, Nebby warmed Lillie's heart by taking her to places where she'd had happy memories—from the beach to her family's favorite restaurant to the room she used to share with her brother. Next, Nebby took Lillie and her friends to another place from her past: the underground entrance to the Aether Foundation. Lillie knew she wasn't allowed in that part of the lab, though, so what were they doing there?

Faba noticed the security breach from his office.

"Oh no!" he worried. "Could she have possibly remembered?"

Meanwhile, in another office at the Aether Foundation, Gladion was upset with their mother, Lusamine. He wanted to know why she ordered Faba to take back Type: Null—but she didn't know what Gladion was talking about! The last Lusamine had heard of Faba's project to develop Type: Null, it was a failure.

"That's not true!" Gladion replied. "Type: Null saved us!"

Gladion explained that four years ago, Faba opened up an Ultra Wormhole right there at the Aether Foundation. An Ultra Beast wrapped its tentacles around Lillie and tried to kidnap her. Luckily, Type: Null jumped to her rescue.

"Lillie totally blocked her memory of the fear she experienced after being attacked by an Ultra Beast," Gladion explained.

Lusamine hadn't known about Lillie's awful encounter with an Ultra Beast, but it certainly explained why she was afraid to touch Pokémon. Together, Gladion and Lusamine headed to Faba's office to rescue Type: Null again.

Meanwhile, Faba was looking for Lillie at the Aether Foundation. He wanted to erase her memory for good, because he was afraid she'd expose his evil deeds. He soon crept up on her.

"How much do you remember now?" Faba asked, grabbing Lillie by the shoulders. "No matter what, you'll forget soon enough."

Faba commanded Hypno to use Hypnosis. Ash's Pikachu tried to stop it with a whack of Iron Tail, but Hypno used Reflect to send Pikachu back.

"Now that it's come to this, I think you should all take a little nap," Faba said. "Hypno, it's time to use Hypnosis!"

In the knick of time, Nebby used Teleport to help Ash and Pikachu dodge naptime. However, Faba had Alakazam toss them back against the wall with a Psychic throw. Then Hypno froze them in place with its Psychic hold. Lillie wriggled free from Faba's grip to try to help her friends, but Alakazam caught her in another Psychic trap and lifted her high up into the air.

Just then, Lusamine and Gladion came running in.

"Lillie!" Lusamine cried, seeing her daughter hovering in midair.

Gladion called upon his pal Type: Null. It arrived with a roar so strong that it burst right out of the helmet Faba built to restrain it. It was truly itself again: the powerful and Legendary Silvally!

"Quick, Silvally! Save Lillie—she's in trouble!" Gladion cried.

Silvally leaped into the air to break Alakazam's Psychic grip on Lillie and carried her safely back to the ground. That sparked Lillie's memory—she remembered that Silvally had saved her in the exact same way from an Ultra Beast. The Pokémon with red eyes in her flashback was not a villain—it was a hero. It was Silvally! Her memory was back!

The battle with Faba was still on. Gladion tossed a shiny disc at Silvally that caught in a special slot on its head.

"Accept this Dark Memory and become the dark beast that brings chaos!" Gladion told the Legendary Pokémon.

Instantly, Silvally transformed into a Dark-type. Then it used a Multi-Attack slash to knock out Alakazam and Hypno. Faba was forced to run.

"Awesome!" Ash said.

Lillie walked up to Silvally, the hero who had saved her twice.

"I remember," Lillie said. "You were the one who rescued me!"

Then she gave Silvally a big hug.

"She's touching it!" Rotom Dex exclaimed.

Snowy, Pikachu, and Nebby all rushed over to give her hugs, too.

"I did it!" Lillie cheered. "I can touch Pokémon! It's absolutely wonderful!"

LEGENDARY & MYTHICAL POKÉMON OF GALAR

WARRIOR
POKÉMON

*HERO OF MANY
BATTLES*

Height
9' 02"

Weight
242.5 LBS.

Type
FAIRY

*CROWNED
SWORD*

Height
9' 02"

Weight
782.6 LBS.

Type
FAIRY-STEEL

ZACIAN

Zacian is one of the pair of brave warriors of the famous hero legend of the Galar region. For a very long time, though, no one even knew of its existence. In fact, if a Trainer came across this Legendary Pokémon, their Pokédex would not recognize Zacian at all.

However, there is no forgetting Zacian's incredible power. Those lucky enough to encounter this Pokémon are always left in awe. Known as a legendary hero, this Pokémon absorbs metal particles, transforming them into a weapon it uses to battle. And when Zacian

HERO OF MANY BATTLES

CROWNED SWORD

possesses the sword it used in the ancient legend, it transforms into Crowned Sword form. Now armed with a weapon it used in ancient times, this Pokémon needs only a single strike to fell even Gigantamax Pokémon. Perhaps that is why it is known as "the Fairy King's Sword."

If Galar is ever cursed again by the return of brutal Eternatus, be sure to summon this Pokémon by heading to its hidden altar in the Slumbering Weald.

HERO OF MANY BATTLES

ZAMAZENTA

Like its partner, Zacian, there was a time when Zamazenta did not appear in a Pokédex. It was unknown, despite the important role it had played long ago in the hero legend of Galar. In times past, it worked together with a king of the people to save the Galar region. It absorbs metal that it then uses in battle.

Zamazenta shares the title of Warrior Pokémon with Zacian, and together they are an unstoppable pair. They possess the perfect balance of a team—which is why even Eternatus fell to Zacian's and Zamazenta's coordinated attack.

It is said that the best offense is a good defense, and that is precisely what makes Zamazenta a force to be reckoned with. When it possesses the ancient shield found at its hidden altar in the Slumbering Weald, Zamazenta transforms temporarily into its Crowned Shield form. With its shield, not even a mighty blow from Eternatus can make it flinch. Those lucky enough to see Zamazenta in action have true admiration for the power of the shield. Its ability to deflect any attack led to it being known as "the Fighting Master's Shield." It was feared and respected by all.

WARRIOR POKÉMON

HERO OF MANY BATTLES

Height
9' 06"

Weight
463.0 LBS.

Type
FIGHTING

CROWNED SHIELD

Height
9' 06"

Weight
1,730.6 LBS.

Type
FIGHTING-STEEL

CROWNED SHIELD

LEGENDARY POKÉMON

GIGANTIC POKÉMON

Height
65' 07"

Weight
2,094.4 LBS.

Type
POISON-DRAGON

ETERNATUS

Twenty thousand years ago, Eternatus was inside a meteorite that landed in Galar. The core on its chest absorbs energy emanating from the lands of the Galar region. This energy is what allows Eternatus to stay active. Because of this connection to Galar Particles, it is thought to also hold the answers to some of the mystery surrounding the Dynamax phenomenon.

When Eternatus is charged up, it becomes very active—and very destructive. It's a force that must be contained, which is easier said than done. Even though Eternatus is gigantic and weighs over a ton, its body is so flexible that it can swirl up into a coil and easily escape capture.

To the people of Galar, Eternatus is better known as the villain in the hero legend, a Pokémon known as the "Darkest Day." However, it was renamed Eternatus by Chairman Rose, the president of the company that supplies Galar with energy. He became obsessed with using its limitless power for his own company's gain.

Since the events in the ancient myth, no one had seen or heard from Eternatus. But that all changed when Chairman Rose restored its power by building a special lab under Hammerlocke Stadium, a Power Spot for precious Galar Particles, so it could regain its strength and resurface.

THE LEGEND OF THE SWORD & THE SHIELD

In the Galar region, certain Pokémon can Dynamax, a phenomenon where they can temporarily grow to be gigantic. Typically, Pokémon can only Dynamax in the Wild Area or stadiums, and their Trainers must wear a special wristband. However, Professor Cerise had lately been hearing reports of Pokémon randomly Dynamaxing and going on rampages across the region. He asked Ash and Goh to travel to Galar to look into the cause and seek out the Dynamax research scientist Professor Magnolia.

On their way, Ash and Goh hopped off the train to chase a Bunnelby, which ended up leading them to the Slumbering Weald. Before they knew it, the dense fog had sent them in totally different directions.

Ash found himself standing before a very unique Pokémon. He whipped out his Rotom Phone, but the Pokédex drew a blank.

"This Pokémon does not match any recorded data," Rotom Phone said.

"No way! A new kind of Pokémon?!" Ash said, examining the majestic creature.

On the other side of the Slumbering Weald, Goh happened upon another unknown Pokémon. Just like Ash, he couldn't believe his luck!

Pokémon Trainers to the core, Ash and Goh were both determined to catch these amazing new Pokémon. Pikachu tried to strike with an Iron Tail slap, but it swung right through the mystery Pokémon.

"Whoa, did you just see that?" Ash said to Pikachu in wonder.

In Goh's neck of the woods, Raboot tried to spark a battle using Ember, but it had the same problem with its attack as Pikachu had.

Who could these unbelievable, untouchable Pokémon be?

Before the two Trainers could get any answers, the two mysterious Pokémon disappeared into thin air!

Ash and Goh found their separate ways out of the woods. They both missed the train, but they both ended up finding a friend. They agreed to keep in touch as their mission took them in different directions.

Ash ended up joining Leon,

Champion of the Galar region. After a Centiskorch had suddenly Gigantamaxed and run amok in a nearby town, Leon had saved the day and successfully snapped it back to its normal state. Then he promised the townspeople he'd find out what was behind the rampaging Pokémon.

Goh had run into his old friend Sonia—who happened to be Professor Magnolia's granddaughter. She was chasing precious Galar Particles that were scattering across the region and was also trying to uncover what was causing the Pokémon to rampage. She and her grandmother Professor Magnolia believed it was linked to the hero legend of Galar, which involves gigantic Pokémon on a rampage. Luckily, the legend has a happy ending: two heroes with a sword and a shield saved Galar from the Darkest Day.

Soon, Professor Magnolia welcomed Goh and Sonia to her lab. She told Goh that she had worked with Chairman Rose—he sponsored young, talented Trainers in the region, like Leon, and he was also the president of Macro Cosmos, a company that developed and supplied energy to Galar. They'd developed the Dynamax Band using the Galar Particles found in Wishing Stars.

"They bring out a power that lies within Pokémon and beckons them to Dynamax," Professor Magnolia said.

She explained that Galar Particles were so dynamic that they might be able to become usable energy for the whole region. She wanted to continue her research on them—but she was afraid of who might misuse it.

"Chairman Rose will stop at nothing when it comes to realizing his dreams," Professor Magnolia warned them. She had a hunch Chairman Rose might be the one behind all the Pokémon Dynamaxing and rampaging.

Next, Sonia and Goh went to visit an ancient mural of the legend. But a secret agent sent by Chairman Rose tried to capture them! He battled Goh, which ended up revealing an old stone statue. It depicted two proud heroes, two unknown Pokémon, and a sword and a shield.

Goh couldn't believe it—one of the Pokémon in the statue looked exactly like the mysterious Pokémon he'd met in the Slumbering Weald!

Goh and Sonia read the statue's inscription. The Legendary Pokémon with the sword in its mouth was Zacian, and the one with the shield was Zamazenta. Goh was certain he'd seen Zamazenta in the Slumbering Weald. He sent Ash a picture of the statue with his Rotom Phone. Could Ash have seen a mysterious Pokémon in the woods, too?

"Whoa! I sure did," Ash confirmed, looking at the statue of Zacian. "That looks just like it!"

Goh and Sonia were now certain the only way to stop the Darkest Day was to find Zacian and Zamazenta. So, the pair headed straight for the Slumbering Weald to ask for their help.

Meanwhile, Leon snuck into Chairman Rose's mine in Hammerlocke because he, too, had a hunch the chairman might be behind the rampaging Pokémon. There he discovered a great golden globe overloaded with Galar Particles—which was about to explode.

"If this keeps up, Eternatus could escape from the hangar!" one of Chairman Rose's agents cried.

"We can't do anything to Eternatus without Chairman Rose's approval!" another agent said.

Now Leon was sure that Chairman Rose was behind the rampaging Pokémon! Worse yet, he was creating the return of the Darkest Day, the Legendary Pokémon called Eternatus.

Suddenly, a huge beam of red light fired into the sky above Hammerlocke Stadium, right above the hangar. Then a claw appeared out of the golden globe—and soon, Eternatus crawled out, growling, and escaped through the top of the mine, into the stadium! Leon feared for the worst as he and Charizard chased after it.

Deep in the Slumbering Weald, Sonia and Goh called out for Zacian and Zamazenta. The Legendary Pokémon heard their cries and appeared. Goh and Sonia told them that the Darkest Day was restored—Galar needed their help again!

Side by side, the two Legendary Pokémon led Goh and Sonia into a thick fog, where they disappeared. But when the fog cleared, before them was an altar that held a sword and a shield.

"They're the ones that appeared in the legend!" Sonia says, putting it all together.

Sonia and Goh knew they were in a race against time to bring the sword and shield to Hammerlocke Stadium.

As Ash and Pikachu swooped into the Stadium on Dragonite, they came face-to-face with Eternatus. It swiftly knocked them to the ground with a roar of bright red light.

"Piikaaaaa," Pikachu whispered, scared.

Chairman Rose had followed Eternatus to the stadium. Proud of his work to revive the Darkest Day, Chairman Rose told Ash and Leon of his evil plan to use the Legendary Pokémon to make energy for his company.

"Eternatus generates limitless Galar Particles. It's the Pokémon of my dreams!" he explained.

"But at the end of each beam, Pokémon Dynamax. And then they start to rampage!" Leon said, pleading with Chairman Rose to change his plan.

"For that very reason, I find talented Trainers like yourself. Now you will catch the revived Eternatus," Chairman Rose told Leon. "Then it will do what I command!"

"Eternatus is too dangerous!" Leon replied.

With a great roar, Eternatus broke through the ceiling of the stadium, into the sky. Hovering below a swirling black cloud, it continued to attract Galar Particles to its core to increase its power.

"The full restoration of Eternatus is near!" Chairman Rose said with delight. "Leon, this is your shining moment."

"I will catch it," Leon vowed. "But then I will seal it away!"

"Do you intend to destroy everything I've worked hard to accomplish?" Chairman Rose yelled, full of rage, then called on Copperajah to stop Leon. Ash and Pikachu stepped in with an Iron Tail wallop to distract Chairman Rose so Leon could sneak away to go after Eternatus.

Suddenly, a massive blast from Eternatus made the entire building rumble—and threw Pikachu to the side.

"Pikachu, no!" Ash cried out. He scooped up his best buddy in his arms. Pikachu was weak and unable to continue battling.

"Use Power Whip!" Chairman Rose commanded his team of Copperajah and Ferrothorn to gang up on Ash and Pikachu. "Finish it!"

But Ash's mighty Riolu jumped in front to protect its friends. It used all its strength to push back against their punches. In the face of such great danger, Riolu's will was so strong that it evolved into incredible Lucario! Now it was even more powerful and fearless. With a double wham of its Aura Sphere, Copperajah and Ferrothorn were left unable to battle.

"You did it, Lucario!" Ash cheered. "Now let's go help Leon."

When Ash found Leon, he was also reunited with his pal Goh. Ash was so excited to see that Goh's Raboot had evolved into Cinderace. They were going to need all the added strength they could get to stop Eternatus!

Leon's Charizard was whipping rounds of Air Slash at Eternatus, and it was finally taking damage.

"That's it!" Leon shouted, encouraging his partner. "Aim your attacks into its mouth!"

While Eternatus looked weakened, Leon boldly tossed a special Ultra Ball to try to catch the strong, dangerous Pokémon. Eternatus slipped into the Poké Ball . . . but seconds later, the Poké Ball burst open, spraying Eternatus's red light all around.

"Look out!" Leon cried, jumping in front of Ash and Goh to protect them.

Leon was badly hurt by the backfire and couldn't continue fighting. The swirling black cloud above the stadium now glowed red. Eternatus rolled its body into the fury. When the glow calmed down, Eternatus reappeared, even bigger and stronger as it took its final form.

From his helicopter, Chairman Rose smiled as he commanded it, "Now, Eternatus, show me your unlimited power!"

Staring right at Ash and Goh, Eternatus let out a massive roar.

"Looks like we're gonna have to stop it!" Ash said.

"Right!" Goh replied.

At once, the sword and shield Goh and Sonia found in the Slumbering Weald lit up.

"All we can do now is become the Legends ourselves!" Goh said, picking up the shield.

"Come on, Eternatus!" Ash and Goh called out.

Goh proudly stated, "For Galar's people and Pokémon . . ."

"We'll stop you right here!" Ash finished.

Ash and Goh's bravery summoned Zacian and Zamazenta from across the region. In a bolt of light, the Legendary Pokémon shot up like arrows into the sky and arrived before Eternatus, ready to battle. With the sword in its mouth, Zacian transformed into Crowned Sword Form with a burst of light. And with the shield in its mouth, Zamazenta became its stunning Crowned Shield Form.

"All right," Ash said with Lucario, Pikachu, and Cinderace by his side. "We'll all do this! We're taking Eternatus down!"

Zamazenta and Zacian leaped straight for the Gigantic Pokémon's head. Red lights popped and fell from Eternatus like fireworks.

"It's taking damage!" Ash said happily.

Cinderace added a scorching Pyro Ball. Lucario sent an intense Aura Sphere. Pikachu fired a shocking Thunderbolt. Eternatus let out a piercing yelp.

"Maybe that means I'll be able to catch it now," Goh hoped.

As Goh took out his Poké Ball, it glowed with white light and grew so big he could barely toss it.

"Poké Ball, go!" Goh shouted, throwing it at Eternatus.

The giant Pokémon again slipped into the Poké Ball . . . but would the ball be able to contain it?

"Eternatus has been registered to your Pokédex," Goh's Rotom Phone confirmed.

Goh had caught Eternatus! Instantly, the swirling cloud in the sky disappeared, revealing a clear night full of stars. Zacian and Zamazenta were gone in a flash.

"Galar has been saved, thanks to all of you!" Leon told Ash, Pikachu, Lucario, Goh, and Cinderace. "I think *you're* the legendary heroes!"

"No way!" Goh replied. "But we do know who they are . . ."

"They're Zacian and Zamazenta!" Ash cheered.

**WUSHU
POKÉMON**

**Height
2' 00"**

**Weight
26.5 LBS.**

**Type
FIGHTING**

KUBFU　　　**URSHIFU**

KUBFU

Kubfu trains hard to perfect its moves. The moves it masters will determine which form it takes when it evolves.

If Kubfu pulls the long white hair on its head, its fighting spirit heightens and power wells up from the depths of its belly.

URSHIFU

Inhabiting the mountains of a distant region, this Pokémon races across sheer cliffs, training its legs and refining its moves.

WUSHU POKÉMON

Height
6' 03"

Weight
231.5 LBS.

Type
FIGHTING-DARK

SINGLE STRIKE STYLE

It's believed that this Pokémon modeled its fighting style on the flow of a river—sometimes rapid, sometimes calm.

RAPID STRIKE STYLE

KUBFU ➡ **URSHIFU**

ZARUDE

MYTHICAL POKÉMON

ROGUE MONKEY POKÉMON

Height
5' 11"

Weight
154.3 LBS.

Type
DARK-GRASS

Within dense forests, this Pokémon lives in a pack with others of its kind. It's incredibly aggressive, and the other Pokémon of the forest fear it.

Once the vines on Zarude's body tear off, they become nutrients in the soil. This helps the plants of the forest grow.

REGIELEKI

This Pokémon is a cluster of electrical energy. It's said that removing the rings on Regieleki's body will unleash the Pokémon's latent power.

Its entire body is made up of a single organ that generates electrical energy. Regieleki is capable of creating all Galar's electricity.

REGIDRAGO

An academic theory proposes that Regidrago's arms were once the head of an ancient dragon Pokémon. The theory remains unproven.

Its body is composed of crystallized dragon energy. Regidrago is said to have the powers of every dragon Pokémon.

GALARIAN ARTICUNO

CRUEL POKÉMON

Height
5' 07"

Weight
112.2 LBS.

Type
PSYCHIC-FLYING

Its feather-like blades are composed of psychic energy and can shear through thick iron sheets as if they were paper.

Known as Articuno, this Pokémon fires beams that can immobilize opponents as if they had been frozen solid.

GALARIAN MOLTRES

MALEVOLENT POKÉMON

Height
6' 07"

Weight
145.5 LBS.

Type
DARK-FLYING

This Pokémon's sinister, flame-like aura will consume the spirit of any creature it hits. Victims become burned-out shadows of themselves.

The sinister aura that blazes like molten fire around this Pokémon is what inspired the name Moltres.

GALARIAN ZAPDOS

STRONG LEGS POKÉMON

Height
5' 03"

Weight
128.3 LBS.

Type
FIGHTING-FLYING

When its feathers rub together, they produce a crackling sound like the zapping of electricity. That's why this Pokémon is called Zapdos.

One kick from its powerful legs will pulverize a dump truck. Supposedly, this Pokémon runs through the mountains at over 180 mph.

GLASTRIER

Glastrier emits intense cold from its hooves. It's also a belligerent Pokémon—anything it wants, it takes by force.

Glastrier has tremendous physical strength, and the mask of ice covering its face is 100 times harder than diamond.

LEGENDARY POKÉMON

WILD HORSE POKÉMON

Height
7' 03"

Weight
1,763.7 LBS.

Type
ICE

SPECTRIER

It probes its surroundings with all its senses save one—it doesn't use its sense of sight. Spectrier's kicks are said to separate soul from body.

As it dashes through the night, Spectrier absorbs the life-force of sleeping creatures. It craves silence and solitude.

LEGENDARY POKÉMON

SWIFT HORSE POKÉMON

Height
6' 07"

Weight
98.1 LBS.

Type
GHOST

LEGENDARY POKÉMON

KING POKÉMON

Height
3' 07"

Weight
17.0 LBS.

Type
PSYCHIC-GRASS

ICE RIDER CALYREX

HIGH KING POKÉMON

Height
7' 10"

Weight
1,783.8 LBS.

Type
PSYCHIC-ICE

SHADOW RIDER CALYREX

HIGH KING POKÉMON

Height
7' 10"

Weight
118.2 LBS.

Type
PSYCHIC-GHOST

CALYREX

Calyrex is a merciful Pokémon, capable of providing healing and blessings. It reigned over the Galar region in times of yore.

According to lore, Ice Rider Calyrex showed no mercy to those who got in its way, yet it would heal its opponents' wounds after battle.

It's said that Shadow Rider Calyrex and a Pokémon that had bonded with it ran all across the Galar region to bring green to the wastelands.

Calyrex is known in legend as a king that ruled over Galar in ancient times. It has the power to cause hearts to mend and plants to spring forth.

It's said that Ice Rider Calyrex once moved a large forest—and all the Pokémon living there—to a new location overnight.

Legend says that by using its power to see all events from past to future, Shadow Rider Calyrex saved the creatures of a forest from a meteorite strike.

LEGENDARY & MYTHICAL POKÉMON OF AN UNKNOWN REGION

MELTAN

Much of what we know about Meltan is thanks to none other than Ash Ketchum and Rotom Dex. Because of their records, Professor Oak was able to name and catalog this Mythical Pokémon.

It all began when a group of Meltan hopped on the ship that carried Ash and his friends to Poni Island in the Alola region. However, they didn't officially meet the Pokémon until some metal tools went missing during a class at the Pokémon School. As it turns out, Meltan have an appetite for anything metal!

Meltan likes the challenge of finding even the tiniest pieces of buried metal. It melts particles of iron and other metals found in the subsoil so it can absorb them into its body of molten steel. It has been known to chew through everything from manhole covers to door handles to even Professor Burnet's frying pan. If something is metal, it's a delicious meal to Meltan!

Though Meltan's body is made of molten steel, it can still be fragile. When Ash's Rowlet tried to save Meltan from Murkrow in midair, it learned that Meltan's precious golden hex nut is not soldered in place—Rowlet caught Meltan's body, but its hex nut fell all the way down to the ground. Luckily, Rowlet was able to help Meltan recover its missing piece, and they have been friends ever since! In fact, because of their friendship, Ash tossed a Poké Ball to catch Meltan, and it joined them on their journey.

MYTHICAL POKÉMON

HEX NUT POKÉMON

Height
0' 08"

Weight
17.6 LBS.

Type
STEEL

MELTAN → **MELMETAL**

MELMETAL

According to Professor Oak, Melmetal and its gifts are celebrated in a handful of ancient texts. Ancient people thought Melmetal was amazing. It is known for a skill that seems like magic: Melmetal can make heavy iron appear out of thin air! And at the end of its life span, Melmetal will rust and fall apart. The small shards left behind will eventually be reborn as Meltan.

The Pokémon disappeared about 3,000 years ago. But by some miracle, the Steel-type Mythical Pokémon has recently returned. In fact, Ash was credited with helping its modern rediscovery, thanks to his pal Meltan's Evolution! Even experts like Professor Oak and Rotom Dex hadn't known that Melmetal was the evolved form of Meltan, but they got to watch it evolve along with Ash, Professor Kukui, and their friends.

The Evolution begins when a single Meltan spins its hex nut, creating a special sound. That sound calls out to dozens of other Meltan in the area, who join in cheering and dancing in circles around that first Meltan. Then bolts of energy ripple through the circles of Meltan until they burst. When the smoke is gone, one giant Melmetal appears.

Right after Ash's Melmetal evolved, it began spinning around and around. Then it swung its fists in super strong punches. Centrifugal force is behind the punches of Melmetal's heavy hex-nut arms—it is said to deliver the strongest punches of all Pokémon. Professor Kukui named this new move the Double Iron Bash. And it was Double Iron Bash that won Ash the round against Professor Kukui and Empoleon in the first Alola League Championships.

HEX NUT POKÉMON

Height
8' 02"

Weight
1,763.7 LBS.

Type
STEEL